REUBEN AND THE BLIZZARD
P. BUCKLEY MOSS, Artist
Story by MERLE GOOD

Good Books
Intercourse, PA 17534 • 800/762-7171
www.goodbks.com

REUBEN AND THE BLIZZARD
Text copyright © 1995 by Good Books, Intercoruse, PA 17534
Art copyright © 1995 by P. Buckley Moss
Design by Dawn J. Ranck
First published in 1995.
New Paperback edition published in 2002.
International Standard Book Number: 1-56148-375-3 (paperback)
International Standard Book Number: 1-56148-184-X (hardcover)
Library of Congress Catalog Card Number: 95-25411

Library of Congress Cataloging-in-Publication Data
Moss, P. Buckley (Pat Buckley)
  Reuben and the quilt / P. Buckley Moss, artist ; story by Merle
Good
  p. cm.
  Sequel to: Reuben and the fire.
  Summary: During a blizzard, Reuben and his Amish family worry
about what to do with their milk, wonder about names for Reuben's
new puppies, help out a neighbor and his pregnant wife, and have fun
sledding near their farm.
  ISBN: 1-56148-184-X (hc.). -- ISBN: 1-56148-375-3 (pbk.)
  [1. Amish--Fiction. 2. Blizzards--Fiction.] I. Moss, P. Buckley (Pat
Buckley), 1933- ill. II. Title
PZy.G5998Rc 1995
[Fic]--dc20   95-25411
                                                      CIP AC

It was the day before the snow came. Reuben was in the barn, trying to decide what to name the five new puppies when his grandfather shuffled in. Dawdi* loved puppies as much as he did.

"They all look like their mother," Dawdi said. And it was true. The tiny pups snuggled up against Spotshine, cozy and half asleep, paying as little attention to Reuben as his five sisters did.

*See final page for pronunciation.

The next day at school, everyone was talking about the snow, as though it were a sure thing. Sam and Ben leaned against the fence during recess, telling Reuben how their dad said it might be a blizzard.

Then the teacher rang the bell, and Reuben and the twins headed back to the schoolroom.

"Did you name those pups yet?" Sam asked.

"It's a secret," Reuben smiled. And they all laughed because they knew that meant Reuben hadn't been able to decide on five new names ending in "shine." He always named his animals that way.

Reuben's younger sister Sadie was up front reciting a poem when Reuben saw the first snowflake. The wind was

blowing hard, and he knew the walk home from school would be a cold one.

By the time they had finished the chores, snow covered the ground. Reuben couldn't even tell where the yard stopped and started. The snow piled up like layers of thick white icing across their farm.

Mamm* and Reuben's sister Mary had fixed a special supper for Dawdi's birthday. Ham loaf and buttered noodles, angel food cake and homemade chocolate ice cream.

Dawdi smiled a lot and told stories about the old days when snow was two feet deep. "It doesn't snow like it used to," Dawdi said. "We used to hitch our horses to the sleigh every winter."

Reuben could hardly remember ever riding in a sleigh.

*See final page for pronunciation.

Before they went to bed, Reuben and Datt* bundled up in their heavy coats and boots and headed out to the barn to check the animals. The cows were asleep, and so were the calves, all looking peaceful in their warm straw.

Spotshine and her puppies slept too, looking like a family. Datt smiled at Reuben and winked. "Do they know their names yet?" he asked.

Reuben smiled back through the heavy scarf wrapped around his neck. "If they do, it's a secret," he said. Datt laughed softly so as not to waken the puppies.

*See final page for pronunciation.

When Reuben came down to the kitchen in the morning, he could barely see the barn, the snow was falling so fast. Datt was out in the howling wind and cold, trying to shovel a path to the cowstable.

Dawdi burst into the kitchen from his end of the house, his eyes big and his voice stronger than usual. "This is like the old days," he said to Mamm by the warm cook stove. Excitement spilled from his voice the way it had on the day the puppies were born.

It snowed all day, the wind whipping white dunes all over the farm and around the buildings. Reuben went to the barn to help with the animals, but he had to take his older sister Annie's hand so he wouldn't get lost in the storm.

When they left the house, they couldn't even see the barn, the snow was so thick in the air. But Annie knew her directions, and a few minutes later they walked against the side of the barn. They followed the wall to the door and stepped into the warm, friendly stable.

"It's the worst snowstorm I've ever seen," Datt said. "I hope we don't have to pour the milk away."

Reuben hadn't stopped to think about what they'd do if the truck from the dairy couldn't get there to pick up the milk. No one liked to waste milk.

Spotshine was glad to see Reuben, but the pups were busy having breakfast, drinking milk from their mother.

Then the wind stopped. The sun came out and no more snow fell.

Reuben stood by the barndoor and looked at the mountains of snow everywhere. He could see Dawdi by the kitchen window, looking out, his eyes big. They waved to each other and laughed.

"What a blizzard!" Datt said. "That has to be more than two feet deep." Reuben knew some of the snowdrifts were higher than his head.

Reuben and all five of his sisters helped their father shovel snow. All day. Even Mamm came out with an old broom. Dawdi wanted to help, but Datt said it wasn't good for his heart.

The roads were closed. The neighbors could not even drive their cars. "It looks like the electric lines are down," Annie said. "I suppose everyone's out of electricity."

But it didn't matter to Reuben's family, because they didn't use electricity. "Sometimes our way has advantages," Mamm smiled.

They were eating a late lunch when Reuben heard a loud knock at their door. It was Lester the Pester from down the road. People called him "the Pester," Mamm used to say, because he played tricks on people.

Lester was worried. His wife Lillie was having a baby and needed to get to the hospital. But the roads were closed and Lester couldn't use his car.

"We'll get out the sleigh," Datt said.

Reuben's heart jumped up and down. He looked at his father with his question, afraid he'd say no.

"If your mother agrees," Datt said.

Lester the Pester fidgeted by the door, as everyone looked at Mamm. Finally she smiled. "You can go along, Reuben," she said, "if you dress warmly. And be careful."

He leaped from the table and went to get his heavy coat.

The sleigh skimmed across the snow like a sled, the horses up ahead, trotting across the fields between the drifts. It was great fun. Lester even laughed. "I can never thank you enough," he said. "I was so worried we couldn't get help."

"Glad to help," Datt said.

Reuben waved at Sam and Ben as the sleigh cut across their fields to Lester and Lillie's house. They were finishing two huge snowmen.

"Look at those snowmen," Lester pointed. "They look like twins!"

They helped Lillie into the sleigh carefully. Then the four of them headed for the main road near town. It was very cold. The sun was setting, throwing light as bright as fire across the frozen snow.

The ambulance met them at the main road. "You did a good thing," the ambulance man with the funny glasses told Datt.

Lillie and Lester thanked them again before the ambulance rushed them away to the hospital.

Reuben found his sister Sadie looking at the pups when he got home. Spotshine licked Reuben's hand as he picked up the pup with the white patch above its nose.

"How are you, Snowshine?" he asked.

Sadie giggled. "May I name one," she begged, "or are they all named already?"

"This one's Frostyshine," he said. "And these two are Whiteshine and Brightshine."

"And what about the last one?" Sadie asked.

"I wasn't sure."

"How about Icingshine?" Sadie suggested.

"Icingshine?"

"Yeah, I thought the snow looked like thick, yummy icing!"

Reuben nodded, and Sadie giggled as she held the pup against her cheek.

That night they had the best sledding Reuben could remember. He and Sadie raced their sleds down the hill behind the barn. Soon his older sisters came out too, laughing and squealing as they whizzed down the snowy tracks.

But what Reuben always remembers about the blizzard was Dawdi on the sled. Dawdi said he wanted one big ride, so he and Reuben piled on the sled together, Dawdi's beard blowing and Reuben laughing. It was such fun, as good as the old days, Reuben guessed. The cold in their faces, everything white, and a ride as fast as the silent wind down the long frozen hill—the two of them together!

How to

(Pennsylvania Dutch

Datt—*(Rhymes*
Mamm—*(Rhymes*
Dawdi—*(Rhymes wi*

There are approximately 150,000 Old————————————ren, living in 22 states and one province of North Amer————————————ical of the Amish in Lancaster County, Pennsylvania

The religious beliefs of the Amish tea————————————dern innovations such as automobiles, electrici————————————ducation. They observe that these modern things oft————————————ships more than they fulfill them. For 300 years, Ami————————————e way," emphasizing family, honesty, basic values

For more information about the Amis————————————P.O. Box 419, Intercourse, PA 17534 (along Route 340), ————————————er (of which Merle Good and his wife Phyllis are Exec————————————f books about the Amish.

About the Artist

P. Buckley Moss (Pat) first met the Amish in 1965 when she and her family moved to Waynesboro in the Shenandoah Valley of Virginia. Admiring the family values and work ethic of her new neighbors, Pat began to include the Amish in her paintings.

Many of her paintings and etchings of both the Amish and the Old Order Mennonites are displayed at the P. Buckley Moss Museum in Waynesboro, which is open to the public throughout the year. For more information, write to: The Director, P. Buckley Moss Museum, 2150 Rosser Avenue, Waynesboro, VA 22980.

Moss and Good collaborated on the earlier classic children's book *Reuben and the Fire.*

About the Author

Merle Good has written numerous books and articles about the Amish, including the beautiful book *Who Are the Amish?* In addition to The People's Place, he and his wife Phyllis oversee a series of projects in publishing and the arts. They live in Lancaster, Pennsylvania, with their two daughters.